THE
LITTLE DRUMMER
MOUSE

THE LITTLE DRUMMER MOUSE

A Christmas Story by Mercer Mayer

SCHOLASTIC INC.

New York   Toronto   London   Auckland   Sydney
Mexico City   New Delhi   Hong Kong   Buenos Aires

ISBN-13: 978-0-545-06226-8
ISBN-10: 0-545-06226-8

12 11 10 9 8 7 6 5 4 3   7 8 9 10 11 12/0

Printed in the U.S.A.   40

First Scholastic printing, December 2007

Text set in Bembo MT Schoolbook

For Autumn Sage Mayer,
our first grandchild

When I first saw you,
I just had to dance.
And, if I was a pony,
I would have to prance.

And, if I played guitar,
I would have to strum.
And, if I was a drummer,
I would have to drum.

But, I am your grandpa,
And, so I wrote a poem.

It had always seemed, for as long as the little mouse could remember, that he followed along behind. He was the smallest in the family and, because it was hard for him to keep up with his brothers and sisters, his mother worried about him a great deal. So she made a tiny drum for him out of a hollow acorn. "My littlest one," she told him, "you are always lagging behind, but at least I'll hear you beating on this drum and that way I won't lose you."

The little drummer mouse, as he came to be called, loved playing on his acorn drum and carried it with him everywhere. But his big brothers and sisters often teased him.

"Pur-rum, pur-rum, pur-rumpety-pum, all you can do is beat your drum," they would chant.

The other forest animals also laughed and teased him. Although the little drummer mouse badly wanted to play with them, he was much too small to join in their rough and tumble games. Instead he would sit under one of the oak trees and beat *tap tap tap* on his little acorn drum.

"What's all that *noise*?" asked a young squirrel. "Don't you know you're supposed to *eat* acorns? My mother told me not to play with my food."

"Go play your drum to the stars. At least you won't bother *them*," added a rabbit.

And so that's just what he did. On clear nights when the mouse family was tucked in bed, the little drummer mouse would often creep outside to the farmer's field. There he loved to watch the stars twinkle back at him as he tapped along, and they even seemed to enjoy his playing as much as he did.

Then one day in autumn, the raven returned to the forest and called to the other animals to gather around. He had astonishing news, for he had heard that the greatest king of all was soon to be born among men. By wintertime the royal family would pass right through this very forest on their way to the town where the baby king would be born.

The excitement in the crowd was so great that the little drummer mouse gave a quick drum roll without even thinking. An old grumpy otter frowned and shushed him.

"We should do something to welcome them," a deer called out, and everyone murmured in agreement.

"You're right," said the wise owl. "We should make the forest beautiful for their journey, and offer gifts to the royal baby."

Everyone said that this made perfect sense, and for weeks they cleaned and decorated the wild forest. Many of the animals brought wonderful gifts for the baby as well.

Then they waited. One morning there came a big snowfall, which covered the forest trees and the farmer's field. But on this cold winter's day very few travelers passed through the forest. There was only a poor man leading a donkey, and a woman wrapped in a thin blanket who rode on the donkey's back. By this time the animals had grown tired of waiting, for it seemed the royal family would never come.

"Well, if this doesn't beat all," said a stylish boar. "And after we've done all this work."

"They have some nerve," added a brown bear.

The animals were all very upset, but the wise owl calmed them down.

"After all," he said, "they're the royal family. No doubt, something of great importance came up and the trip was canceled."

That cheered everyone up, and since they had prepared a grand celebration, they had a wonderful party anyway. They danced and sang and ate until the sun set and the first stars of evening twinkled in the heavens above.

Later, snug in his bed, the little drummer mouse was still too excited to sleep. Looking out the little window in the bedroom he shared with his many brothers and sisters, he noticed a new bright star that shone down from heaven. It was the most beautiful star he had ever seen. Quietly he took his acorn drum and crept out to the field to get a better look.

He was so intent on watching the star that he didn't notice three tall figures crossing the field in his direction.

"Young mouse," said a sudden deep voice. "We are looking for a stable. Is there one nearby?"

The little mouse turned and trembled with fear at the three men who towered over him.

"Who . . . who are you?" stammered the little mouse.

The one in blue spoke. "We are three kings from far away, seeking a child born in a stable beneath this star. This child will be a great king, even greater than us."

"But how can that be?" asked the little drummer mouse, being very brave. "Kings aren't born in stables."

"This one was," said the tallest king. "Now, will you tell us if there is a stable nearby?"

The little mouse pointed the way. The three kings thanked him, and he watched as they walked away, followed by the strangest animals he had ever seen. Upon their backs were large humps and upon the humps were chests of treasure.

I wish I could see the baby king, thought the little drummer mouse. *Perhaps I will just peek, and no one will notice me since I am so small.* Pulling his courage together the little mouse set off after the three kings.

The stable was not much more than a shed, but it was warm. As the little drummer mouse squeezed through a crack in the wall he saw a crowd of farmers and shepherds. He watched as each person stepped forward to lay something shabby and simple before a manger. Over the manger stood the man and the woman who had passed through the forest the day before.

Then the three tall kings came forward to give their rich and beautiful gifts. There was gold and silver, and perfumes that smelled wonderful.

So it is true, thought the little mouse. *He must indeed be a great king. I'd better be going. After all, I haven't been invited and I have nothing to give.* He tried to creep back out through the crack, but a shepherd's foot was blocking the way.

The shepherds began to play a tune on their harps and flutes. The sound was so lovely that the little drummer mouse began to tap along on his acorn drum. He became lost in the magic of the song and didn't notice when the other musicians fell silent.

The baby had awakened, and the young mother lifted him from the manger. She turned toward the little mouse, who was still tapping, and said, "Bring forth the drummer and raise him up so that he may see."

Suddenly two large hands scooped him up. The little drummer mouse cringed in terror. But to his surprise the woman smiled at him and said, "You, tiniest of all, keep playing your little drum. The baby seems to like that sound the best."

The little drummer mouse looked at the baby and the baby laughed. Then he began to play again, slowly at first, then a little faster. Everyone listened and smiled, and he could have shouted for joy. The flute chimed in, followed by the harp. Soon everyone in the stable joined along, playing and singing a beautiful song.

For the first time ever the little drummer mouse with his little acorn drum wasn't being teased or following along behind. He was leading instead.